# HOLD ME DOWN
## *Hard*

A BREAKING THE RULES NOVELLA

# CATHRYN FOX

Entangled Publishing, LLC
644 Shrewsbury Commons Ave
STE 181
Shrewsbury, PA 17361
rights@entangledpublishing.com

Brazen is an imprint of Entangled Publishing, LLC.

Edited by Libby Murphy and Theresa Cole
Cover design by Heather Howland
Cover art from iStock

Manufactured in the United States of America

First Edition May 2013

ENTANGLED
BRAZEN

*I have so many people to thank for my first book at Entangled Publishing. First, thanks to Theresa Cole and Libby Murphy for helping me make this story shine! You both rock! Secondly, thank you to Jan Meredith for sharing so much with me and always believing in me. And last but not least, thanks to my daughter, Allison, for always supporting me and for making me laugh when I need to the most.*

# Chapter One

Eden Carver dealt the remaining cards from the deck and glanced at her three friends as they gathered around her small kitchen table for their weekly game of poker. She took note of the nearly empty glasses and made a move to get up.

"Anyone want another…" Her voice fell off when the sound of her neighbor's Jeep pulling into their shared parking lot drew her attention.

She dropped back into her chair and noted the warm shivers of delight raining down her spine as she strained to hear her best friend's footfalls on the stairs. The echo of his size-twelve boot hitting the first step quickened her breath. As she listened, there was nothing she could do to keep her pulse from racing, nothing she could do to prevent her nipples from pressing insistently against her thin white tank top.

"Hello, earth to Eden," Janie said, waving her arms in front of Eden's face to pull her attention back to the game at hand.

As a humid summer breeze fluttered the lacy curtains over her sink, Eden blinked her mind back into focus and met

Janie's shrewd glance. While the four girls sitting around the table were all actresses, having met on a movie set after Eden moved to the Big Apple three years ago, Janie was by far the most flamboyant and loudest of the bunch.

Eden shook her head. "Sorry, where was I?" she asked, with only half her attention on her cards. The other half was still on her neighbor and how she'd do just about anything to get a glimpse of him in his police uniform before he peeled it from his rock-hard body and called it a night.

God, if he only knew what it did to her, knew how many times she'd lain in bed and conjured naughty scenarios with the big bad cop in his work wear—doing delicious things to her with his cuffs—he'd surely think she was a deviant and run the other way. This, of course, was the main reason she'd never admit her desires to anyone. Not ever again, anyway. The one time she'd told a guy how she felt about men in uniforms, the way her mind's eye played out a bevy of kinky fantasies— like being shackled to the bed or tied at the ankles—he'd run straight into the arms of a *normal* girl. Apparently, because she was from Iowa, he, as well as everyone else, expected her to be a shy country girl, not some wild and twisted pervert— which was what he'd called her on the way out of her condo and out of her life.

But dammit, she was tired of hiding the real Eden, and she wanted a guy she could be herself with, a guy who accepted her for who she was and who wasn't afraid to explore all her darkest desires.

Except it wasn't just *any* guy with whom she wanted to share her wicked side. Oh no, not at all. The guy she wanted to lay herself bare to was none other than her best friend, Jay Bennett.

"Oh. My. God," Maria whispered, her big blue eyes bulging wide as she studied Eden. When Maria's mouth dropped open, her chin dangling inches from the table, Eden feared her friend was about to catch the fly buzzing around the kitchen.

Angie picked up her strawberry daiquiri and gave a small salute to Maria. "Oh my God is right."

"What?" Eden asked, working to keep a measure of calm as all three glared at her like they could see straight into her soul. Then again, they'd all shared so much over the last few years that maybe they could. Maybe they knew how much she wanted her neighbor, in and out of his uniform.

Janie snapped her fingers and did some weird head-bobbing thing before saying, "You've got it bad, girlfriend."

Eden stared at her friends for a moment longer, then let loose a long-suffering sigh, deciding any attempt to hide her feelings from the trio, who probably knew her better than she knew herself, was simply an exercise in futility.

"I know," Eden admitted and buried her face in her hands. "I've got it bad. But he totally friend-zoned me. He's not interested in sharing anything more than pizza and movies."

The truth was, while she wanted a shot at a real relationship with her best friend, one that would eventually involve a white picket fence and a brood of kids, he seemed more than happy with the way things were between them. She loved hanging out with him, loved how he checked in on her every night, and especially loved lounging on the sofa and sharing a bowl of popcorn during one of their many weekend movie marathons. But as much as she pried, Jay never opened up on a deeper personal level and never shared his work life with her, even when she knew he'd had a bad day and needed to vent.

Maria frowned. "Are you sure he doesn't have a girlfriend somewhere?"

"Positive."

Janie arched an inquisitive brow. "Maybe he just isn't commitment material." She rolled her eyes and added,

"Typical playboy."

"You could be right," Eden said, nodding in dismay.

Maria blinked dark lashes over hopeful eyes. "Maybe you could reform him. Prove to him you're the one and only girl for him."

Eden blew an exaggerated breath. While she would love to do just that, she wasn't sure how to go about it. Nor was she even sure *if* she could tame him, considering the amount of women she'd seen coming and going from his place over the last three years. Maybe he just wasn't interested in long-term with anyone.

"Yeah," Angie said. "*Show* him just how good you two can be together."

"How? We're friends and he just doesn't seem interested in anything more."

"Then *make* him interested," Janie said.

Eden planted her elbow on the table and rested her forehead in her palm. "Make him? How am I supposed to do that?"

"He helps you rehearse your scripts, right?"

"Yeah. What does that have to do with anything?"

Across the table from her, Maria giggled and shared a conspiratory look with Janie. Janie winked at her as Angie reached over and pulled Eden's palms from her face and handed her a much-needed drink.

"It has everything to do with it," Maria said.

Wondering what she was missing, Eden took a big sip of her daiquiri and leaned back in her chair. "You two want to enlighten me?"

Janie rolled her big brown eyes and her voice was teasing when she asked, "God, Eden, do I have to spell everything out for you?"

"Apparently."

"Get your ass over there right now and ask him to help

you rehearse."

Frustrated, Eden threw her arms up in the air. "He runs lines with me all the time and it's never made him notice me before. What makes you think this time will be any different?"

Janie leaned forward, a mischievous grin curling her painted lips. "Because this time, sweet, naïve Eden, you're going to write the script."

Eden exhaled slowly and sank a little lower in her chair. Even though she couldn't believe what her friend was suggesting, it didn't stop her salacious mind from racing with devious plots, ones that involved Jay in his sexy uniform rescuing and cuffing an innocent—or not so innocent— damsel in distress.

Her gaze shifted to Angie, the most logical and rational thinker of the bunch, but when Angie pointed one manicured finger toward her door and gave her an encouraging smile, Eden's thoughts once again careened in an erotic direction.

Shivers of anticipation trickled along every vertebra in her spine as she thought about playing out the role she'd been fantasizing over for months. Her breath came in shallow bursts and a low, needy moan lodged deep in her throat when her eyes strayed toward her door. She blew a wispy strand of hair from her face as basic elemental need took over, urging her to heed her friends' advice and show Jay how good they could be together both in and out of the bedroom. Her body trembled almost uncontrollably as she visualized herself going over to his condo with her very own sexy script—before he climbed out of his uniform.

But it was so risky. So outrageous. So downright naughty.

Then again, hadn't she just said she wanted a real relationship with Jay, wanted him to like her for who she was? Five minutes ago, she swore she would never share her secret fantasies with anyone, but wasn't this the perfect way to show him the real Eden—to let him see the naughty beneath the nice — and show him how they could be together? Plus, she also wanted Jay, a guy who risked his life every day to serve others, to really open up to her and share all aspects of his life.

Feeling restless, needy, and oh-so-edgy, she took a moment to give the wicked scheme further consideration. Less than a heartbeat later, as she warmed to the idea of seducing the bad-ass cop next door, ribbons of desire pulsed in her blood and she fought the urge to squirm in her seat. But then worry hit like a sucker punch when she thought more about their friendship.

What if her seduction and secret fetishes ruined their relationship?

What if they didn't?

# Chapter Two

Jay stopped at the top of the landing and turned toward Eden's door. He was about to knock, but when he heard voices coming from inside he remembered it was Thursday night, which meant it was girls' night out, or in this case, girls' night in. Disappointment settled in his gut as he shoved his hands into his pockets. Turning on the balls of his feet, he made his way to his own condo across the hall.

The officer in him liked to check in on his neighbor on a nightly basis. After all, Eden might think she was a seasoned New Yorker, but he knew she was just a sweet and innocent Iowa farm girl deep inside, one who was a bit naïve when it came to the dangers of the big city. The man in him, however, liked to check in on the girl next door for entirely different reasons. Selfish reasons.

*Eden...*

Like the name, she was pure paradise. But as tempting as she was, he knew if he took one small bite, nothing good would come from it. He definitely wasn't the guy for her because at the end of the night, she deserved to crawl between the sheets with a lover who was slow and gentle. Not with a guy who wanted to ravish her with dark hunger over and over again. And he was pretty sure if he ever got her naked, there was no other way he could give it to her.

Even though he knew he was all wrong for her, it still didn't stop him from wanting to hang out with her every weekend. During the week, before hitting the sack, he loved to see her pretty face, her soft curvy body, and that sexy mouth that dreams were made of. In fact, he looked forward to their exchanges in the hallway. There was something so arousing and alluring in the way her big, honey-flecked eyes lit up when he checked in on her. It gave him something to think about other than the corrupt world in which they lived—a world he had every intention of protecting Eden from.

Moments before he reached his condo door, her voice drifted into the hallway and seeped under his skin. Jesus, his cock thickened just from the sound of her sweet laughter. But it wasn't like sex between them was going to happen, because when it came to Eden, there was a line he wasn't going to cross.

They were good friends, which meant he wasn't going to let his lust get the better of him, no matter how much he wanted her.

No, he intended to keep her safe and alive and out of his dangerous world, something he hadn't been able to do for his kid sister, Jess, when they were both teens. His hand went to the tattoo of her name and he thought about the reason behind his career choice. Even if he wanted a deeper relationship with Eden, he knew he couldn't have it. Eventually, she'd want him to quit the streets. He'd seen it happen to dozens of guys at the precinct, and if he took a desk job he'd be betraying the memory of his sister. After he'd lost her, he vowed to become a cop and crack down on gang fighting in the downtown core. Her death would not be in vain.

Jay shoved the key into his lock and pushed open his door. He stepped inside his small condo and when he flicked on the lights, an instant pang of loneliness hit like a slap in the face — a reminder that he hadn't dated or brought another woman back to his place in a few weeks.

He glanced at the contact list on his iPhone as he shrugged out of his jacket and unbuttoned his shirt. But instead of making a call and engaging in meaningless sex, he grabbed a cold beer from his fridge and plunked himself down on the sofa to watch some mind-numbing TV. He flicked through the stations until he came across Eden's favorite reality show, then looked at the empty seat beside him, wishing she was there.

Not wanting to think about how empty the place felt without his sexy neighbor there to brighten it up, he took another slug of his beer, set it on his coffee table, and made his way to the shower.

He stayed under the hot spray for a good long time, until the water turned cold and he heard someone pounding insistently on his condo door.

Without drying his body, he whipped the towel off the hook next to the shower and tied it around his waist. "Okay, I'm coming," he bellowed. Jesus, was there some kind of emergency going on in his hallway?

He rushed to his front door and flung it open. His heart picked up tempo when he came face-to-face with Eden. He was about to smile until he noticed the strange look on her face, one he'd never seen before and couldn't quite identify. His heart dropped into his stomach.

He grabbed her, hauled her inside, and looked past her shoulders into the empty hallway. "What's going on? Are you okay?"

She nodded, and he gave her a once-over before he closed the door and locked it. His eyes traveled back to her face and when he spotted the slight pink hue on her cheeks as she blatantly stared at his bare chest, he suddenly became very aware of his clothes, or lack thereof.

"I've caught you at a bad time," she said, her voice a touch lower than usual.

"I was in the shower. I thought there was an emergency."

Eden nibbled her bottom lip, and while her look was apologetic, he thought he spotted a glimmer of vulnerability before she said, "I should go."

"No, you should stay." He gave her a playful grin and, hoping to lighten her mood and put a smile on her pretty face, he added, "And you should tell me what's so important that you nearly knocked my damn door down."

Her eyes cast down for a brief moment and he could sense her trepidation, the apprehension brewing just beneath the surface.

Worry moved through him. He'd never seen her like this before and, as a police officer who'd seen some pretty bad shit, his mind went down a dark path, one that brought back painful memories of the night his sister got killed.

"Did someone hurt you?" He fisted his hands and briefly glanced at his closed door, ready to tear it from its hinges and hunt down whoever dared to harm her.

"No, it's not that," she answered quickly.

Working to keep calm, he put his finger under her chin and tilted her face until they were eye-to-eye. "Tell me what's wrong."

She looked at him for a long moment, then he felt a shift inside her, felt her body relax under his scrutinizing gaze.

"Well," she began, returning to her warm, sexy self as she waved a script in front of his face. "I was wondering if you could run lines with me. There's a part I want to play and it's very, very important that I get it right. It could mean all the difference for my future."

He exhaled a breath. "Oh. Okay." He took the script from her and passed off her odd behavior as nothing more than the burning need to land a new role. "What's the part you're going for?"

"It's the lead role, which is why I have to nail both the lines and the character."

Something in the way she said *nail* brought heat to his body and his mind went down a path it had no right to go. Jay cleared his throat, plunked himself down on the sofa, and worked to get his mind on the script and off the way Eden's blouse clung to her full breasts.

Eden smoothed down her short, sexy skirt and sat next to him. Her long blond hair tumbled in silken waves over her shoulders and when she shimmied in close, her sweet, familiar scent reached his nostrils. Lust instantly bombarded his body and there was nothing he could do to stifle the low growl of longing crawling out of his throat.

"Are you okay?"

She leaned toward him, and the position afforded him a perfect view of her lush cleavage. He tried to look away. He really did. But God dammit, this farmer's daughter had a body made for sin. With his cock thickening and his mouth salivating for a taste of her, eager for one tiny nibble, his glance traveled back to her face. He could have sworn he saw mischief in her eyes before she quickly blinked it away. But he had to be mistaken. The Eden he knew didn't play sexual games.

"Are you okay?" she asked again.

"Yeah, I'm fine."

Jay cleared his throat a second time and it took every ounce of concentration he had to read over the lines. After quickly scanning the pages and realizing she wanted him to play out a sexy damsel-in-distress scene, one that involved hot kissing and intimate touching, his cock grew another inch. He shifted, suddenly uncomfortable, and that's when he noticed his towel sporting a telltale pup tent.

*Fuck.*

He jumped to his feet and turned away to hide the bulge before Little Jay poked his head out and grabbed a front-row seat for the upcoming show. Dropping the script onto his coffee table, he inched backward.

"I…uh…I should probably get dressed."

When his dry throat cracked, he reached for his bottle of beer and took a drink before handing it to Eden. She put the bottle to her mouth for a long, slow sip. He watched her, watched the way her lush lips wrapped around the long, smooth neck, and even though they'd drunk from the same bottle many times before, tonight there seemed to be something very intimate in the way they were sharing.

She lowered the bottle and swiped her tongue over her bottom lip. The action was so damn sexy it was all he could do to keep it together. She stretched out on his sofa and his brain took that moment to go on a sensual adventure, his lust-saturated mind visualizing the way he'd like to caress her body.

"I was thinking," she began, the seductive lilt in her voice pulling his thoughts back and turning him inside out. "The male lead in the script is a cop, so maybe you should put your uniform on to really help me get into the role." She paused for a moment, and there was a strange hitch to her voice when she added, "And don't forget the handcuffs."

When he looked at her and thought about what she was asking of him, the scene she wanted him to play out, his first instinct was to run the other way. But if the role was this important to her, then it was important to him, too, and he certainly couldn't turn away from her when she needed him, no matter how much torture he was about to put himself—or Little Jay—through.

No, he would never leave her hanging. She'd asked for a favor and he was a man who'd vowed that he'd always be there for her. But the question was: how could he possibly practice such a titillating scene without taking a small nibble for himself?

After all, Eden was pure temptation.

And a man could only resist temptation for so long.

# Chapter Three

Eden drew a breath to center herself as she waited for Jay to return. After her friends had left, their encouraging words still echoing in her brain, she'd changed into sexy clothes, not to mention her favorite stilettos, but there was a part of her that could hardly believe she was actually going to go through with such a devious plan.

When Jay had first opened the door and she'd set eyes on his half-naked body, all wet and sexy from his recent shower, she'd felt a brief moment of hesitation and wondered if she was biting off more than she could chew. The man was smoking hot and if things went according to her plan, then after tonight life as they both knew it would be forever altered.

She was hoping her seduction would bring the two of them closer, to show him how good they could be together, but there was still a small part of her that feared it could tear their friendship apart—that he would think she was some sort of sexual deviant and run the other way. But how could she possibly continue to go on dreaming and fantasizing about a future with Jay without doing something about it? No, she had to do this. She had to show him the real Eden Carver and get him to notice her as something more than a pizza-and-movie pal.

"So, what do you think?" Jay asked, his deep, sexy voice curling her toes as he came back into the room.

Eden glanced at him and he shifted from one foot to the other, like he was uncomfortable but trying to hide it. A fine shiver moved through her as she took in his starched uniform and she had to bite back a moan of want when she noticed the way his shirt and pants hugged his sculpted body so flawlessly. He came closer and the rich scent of his freshly showered skin, combined with the aroma of fabric softener, had her hungering for him with an intensity that was almost frightening.

He widened his arms so she could examine him and that's when she noticed the handcuffs. "Do I fit the lead male role?"

Oh, he fit it all right. He just had no idea how well.

"It was almost like it was written for you," she answered, hoping her voice didn't sound as mischievous as she felt.

Jay picked up his script and frowned. "I've never known you to take on such a racy role before."

"A girl's gotta stretch her acting muscles every now and then."

"Actually, these lines seem a bit cheesy."

Eden crinkled her nose and tried not to take offense. She was an actress, not a screenwriter for heaven's sake, and the whole scenario played out much better in her head than it did on paper.

He flipped the page and read on. "Jesus, it reads like a bad porn movie. The main character likes to be tied up, spanked, and has all kinds of fetishes, like BDSM and exhibitionism." He pulled a face. "She even wants her ex-lover to have sex with her in the alleyway. Are you sure you want this role?"

"I'm sure once we get into character and add the emotions,

it will sound better." With that she gave an efficient clap of her hands and said, "Okay, let's take our places and pick up where the heroine finds herself cornered in a dark alleyway by two thugs. This is where you enter, scare the guys off, and come to her rescue."

She watched his throat work as he swallowed. His voice came out a little rough, a little edgy when he asked, "Isn't that the part where she seduces him?"

"Yeah," she agreed, "it's the part I'm having the hardest time nailing. So I thought we should pick it up there."

Slipping into the role of damsel in distress, Eden mussed her hair and opened a few buttons on her blouse to make it look like she'd been fighting off her attackers.

Once she was ready, she pressed her back to the wall and gestured for Jay to come close. He glanced at the script, then back at Eden as he closed the distance, and an agonized look came over his face when he positioned himself in front of her, his body pinning hers against the wall.

"Did they hurt you?" he asked as he got himself into character for her.

"They tried, but I was able to fight them off."

They ran through the next few lines, and she hurried them to the spot where he kissed her. She put on her best sultry face and said, "I miss seeing you in your uniform." She paused, traced her tongue over her lips, and added, "And I miss seeing you out of it."

With his lips hovering over hers, everything in the way he had her caged with his chest to the way he was staring at her mouth generated heat inside her.

Prompted by need, she aligned her hips with his and pressed her sex against his groin. The movement was slight, but from the tortured look on Jay's face and the way his entire body stiffened, she knew he'd felt it.

Looking like he was in sheer agony, Jay dropped the

script onto the floor and planted his hands on either side of her head. His voice came out a little broken, a little labored when he shifted his stance and asked, "Uh, so this is where I kiss you?"

She worked to find her voice. "Yeah," was all she could manage to get out. Good God, she was down to one-word answers and if he didn't do something soon she was going to explode into a million pieces.

When she met his glance, sexual tension arced between them, and she was certain anyone within a fifty-mile radius could feel the tremendous heat they were creating inside his condo.

Jay swiped his tongue over his bottom lip. "So I...uh...I guess I should kiss you now."

Her entire body quivered in heated anticipation, because this was the moment she'd been fantasizing about for so damn long now. She knew he was waiting for a reply, but since words were beyond her, she nodded, and when he dipped his head, bringing them eye-to-eye, ripples of sensual pleasure danced along her skin.

She poised, her mouth open, conveying without words what she wanted, but when he gave her a quick, jerky peck on her mouth, his lips barely scraping hers, a chaotic lump settled deep in her gut and she nearly sobbed from disappointment.

Maybe he really just wasn't interested.

As she mulled that over, she listened to the pounding of his heart, and that's when she noticed the way his breath was coming in quick, shallow bursts. He moved restlessly, and she took that moment to steal a downward glance. The second she spotted the huge bulge in his sexy work pants, hope surged inside her.

Okay, so maybe he *was* interested, and maybe she was simply going about this all wrong.

With her mind racing a million miles an hour, she pushed

him away. Deciding to change tactics, she dropped down onto the sofa and with renewed purpose she said, "This isn't working. I can't quite capture the emotions in the role. My character is supposed to be in grave danger before getting rescued by her former lover, and I'm just not feeling it."

He almost looked relieved as he raked a shaky hand through his hair. "You want to call it a night?"

Eden crinkled her nose and knew she had to shake things up. She had to get him out of his comfort zone and into a place where he'd forget they were running lines and give in to his urges.

"Actually, I was thinking we could take it outside. You know, so we can recreate the scene in a dark alleyway, put ourselves in the situation, and really get into character."

He gave a quick shake of his head. "It's almost midnight, and I don't want you in a dark alleyway by yourself. The city streets are dangerous."

"I won't be by myself. You'll be there with me. And you're not going to let anything happen to me, are you?"

That earned her a scowl. "Do you even have to ask?"

"No, I don't. So I guess it's settled then. Let's take this show on the road, shall we, and see what we can come up with."

· · ·

Jay knew exactly what he could come up with. A rock hard erection, that's what.

*Fuck.*

Even though he'd sworn he would never cross the line with her, the minute she'd pressed her soft, sensual body against his, his dick had hardened to the point of pain. And when she'd gyrated, aligning her hips with his, it had taken all his effort to keep his hard-on under wraps, although he was beginning to believe he hadn't quite accomplished that task. When she'd glanced between their bodies, he was pretty damn sure she'd glimpsed his traitorous cock. How could she not, considering the insistent way it was pressing against his unforgiving work pants?

Before he could tell her it wasn't settled, she scooped up the script, tucked it under her arm, and bolted out the door.

"Come on, let's go."

With his lust-rattled brain hardly able to keep up, he called out to her, struggling to find a way to help her without reenacting a sexy scene in the alleyway, but she'd already picked up the script and was halfway down the stairs before he could stop her.

"Dammit," he cursed, and hurried after her.

By the time he caught up, she was already outside the building. With determination etched on her face, she headed to the small alleyway that separated their condo complex from the identical building beside it.

"Come on," she said, waving him in.

"I don't know."

She frowned. "Okay, if you're not up to it, I guess I can ask Mike Douglas from down the hall."

An unwise pang of jealousy hit and there was nothing he could do to bank it. As an actress, she must kiss different men all the time. He understood that was part of her job, but the thought of her kissing Mike didn't sit well with him, especially since he saw the hungry way Mike always looked at her.

"Fine," he conceded halfheartedly, looking into the alleyway. At least they were in a safe neighborhood and not downtown where it was dangerous, and since he was in his work wear, if anyone happened upon them they'd either think he was a cop in the line of duty or getting his kink on with his girlfriend. "Let's just get this done."

"Okay," she said as she toyed with her top button, her

glance darting around to check the location as she got herself into the role. When she looked back at him, her smile was more seductive than sweet and suddenly, all he could think about was nailing her against that wall and taking her hard and fast.

But this was sweet Eden Carver. Even though she tempted him in mind-fucking ways, he was here to help her run lines, not hold her down hard and fuck her.

"Why don't we pick this up at the beginning?" She gestured with a nod toward the parking lot. "Go out there and wait for my signal."

Moonlight spilled over them, giving him sufficient light to see her features but not enough to see the small print on the script. "It's dark, and I won't be able to read my lines."

She paused for a moment, and he hoped she was thinking about calling it off.

She dropped the script. "Why don't you just follow my lead?" she finally suggested, and if he wasn't mistaken there was something very sensual and suggestive in her eyes as they moved over his uniform. "As long as I read mine correctly, you should be able to respond like any cop would. You know, just wing it. Do and say what comes naturally."

He was about to protest again, to tell her that probably wasn't a good idea—for reasons he couldn't quite admit—but she waved him away and began getting herself into character, the way he'd watched her do numerous times in the past when he'd helped her rehearse.

"Fine," he conceded unenthusiastically, only because this was so important to her. He twisted on the balls of his feet and walked away from her. The warm night air moistened his skin and he scrubbed a shaky hand over his face as he left Eden to get into character.

He, too, needed to get into character and summon all his control to try to get through this scene without tearing the clothes from her body, save for those high heels, and ravishing her—caveman style.

He stood near his Jeep and as he waited for her signal, he wondered what was taking her so long. Was it possible that she was having second thoughts about rehearsing such a sexy scene with him? After all, this provocative role was a real stretch for her. And maybe he'd mistaken her nervousness earlier. Maybe she had concerns about what she was asking him—a friend—to do and less about her apprehension over getting the role.

He tossed that idea around in his mind and hoped like hell he'd gotten off lucky and she'd changed her mind about all this. When she called out to him, he frowned. Guess not.

He rushed to the mouth of the alleyway, but when he saw her, saw the way she looked so mussed and sexy, blood pounded through his veins and knocked him off-kilter. He braced his hand on the wall beside him and worked to stifle the emotions and sensations bombarding him as he took in the gorgeous woman waiting for him to come to her rescue.

In the moonlit alleyway her eyes met his, big wide saucers full of surprise and relief. "Officer," she rushed out, a note of desperation in her voice as she followed the scripted lines. "They went that way." She turned her head and pointed to the opposite end of the passageway.

"Did they hurt you?" he asked, remembering his next line as he did his best to get into character for her.

*But by God, she looks sexy.*

"They tried, but I was able to fight them off."

"You were very brave," he said, pitching his voice low as he closed the distance between them, but when he moved into her personal space, she gasped and regarded him with wide eyes.

"It's you."

"Yeah, it's me," Jay said and glanced up and down the

alleyway to check for danger before he asked, "What are you doing out here alone?"

She pushed her blond curls off her face and gave a defiant tilt of her head, like she knew a lecture was coming. As he watched her play out the scene, lust mingled with pride, because he realized just how good she was at this, just how believable and convincing she could be when she put her mind to it.

"I had a late shift at the hospital and I was in a hurry to get home."

He stood before her and dipped his head until their gazes clashed. "How many times do I have to tell you it's not safe to take shortcuts?"

When he took a measured step closer, his body crowding hers like the script demanded, it triggered a reaction in her. He felt a tremble move through her as her hand reached out to surf along his jaw. He put his large palm on the small of her back to drag her closer, and that's when he realized that the scene they were rehearsing was so damn familiar to the fantasies he'd had about her. Her fingers tracked lower to slide along his stiff collar and, from the way she was looking over his attire, he'd hazard a guess that her character also had some sort of uniform fetish.

She leaned into him and when her nipples scorched his chest, he didn't miss the intimacy of what they were doing. Even though they were acting, and a level of separation existed between the characters they were playing and the man and woman currently facing each other, there was nothing impersonal in the way they were touching.

Her expressive eyes devoured him with raw need and a low moan sounded in her throat, a soft, sexy bedroom noise that raised his hunger to dangerous proportions.

Her voice was nothing more than a seductive whisper and held all kinds of innuendoes—all kinds of promises—when she said, "You never were one for shortcuts were you, Riley?"

Want exploded inside him and he swallowed. Hard. Riley might be the character he was playing, and even though she'd called him by many different names when they ran lines, tonight it sounded odd coming from her lips. Tonight—God help him—he wanted her to call him Jay. Wanted her to look at *him* like that. Wanted this to be real.

*Get it together, Bennett.*

He drew a fueling breath and reminded himself that he wasn't going to cross the line with her. Not only that, if he took her the way he wanted, what would happen to their friendship? He couldn't risk losing her from his life.

"Actually," she murmured, a new kind of urgency and emotion in her voice. "Even though I know you're going to give me a lecture, I'm glad it was you who came to my rescue."

"Why's that?"

Warm heat moved over her eyes, and when she adjusted her stance and rubbed up against him like a cat scratching an itch, he knew he was in a shitload of trouble.

"Because I've missed you," she said, her hands circling his shoulders to hold him tight. When her body pressed against his, all he could think about was stripping her naked and having his way with her. He ached to drink in her sensuous body, to lick a path down her flesh until he reached the spot his mouth craved the most.

Feeling edgy and fearing his lust was about to overtake him, he eased back, pulled in a fortifying breath, and asked, "What did you miss about me?"

As soon as he put an inch of distance between them, she gave a frustrated sigh. "It's still not working."

Jay swallowed, because whatever it was they were doing here was damn well working for him. Christ, he was hurting so badly his cock was about to burst through his pants.

She made a sexy sound and shifted closer. "Maybe I

should rip open my blouse, you know, to really help me get into character."

His heart began racing. "You want to rip open your blouse?"

"Yeah, the script said my clothes were practically torn from my body."

When her hand went to her blouse, he shackled her wrists and put his mouth close to her ear. "I'm not so sure that's a good idea."

She frowned. "I need to nail this part, and I think it would really help."

There was that word again, the one that suggested all kinds of erotic possibilities. Commanding himself to get it together and remembering how important this was to her, he let go of her and with one quick yank, she tore it open. Her buttons scattered to the ground, and when he set eyes on her lacy black bra, his brain stalled and his body reacted with urgent need.

"Riley," she said.

He struggled to find his voice. "Who's Riley?"

She gave a low, throaty chuckle. "You are, remember?"

Hell no, he didn't remember.

She blinked up at him. "The next line is yours."

Christ, he couldn't remember his own name let alone his next line.

"You have to ask me what I missed about you," she said, coming to his rescue.

Working to keep a measure of calm, he pressed his hands on either side of her head again, and with his scripted words long forgotten, he asked, "What did you miss about me?"

She ran her hand along his chest, her fingers toying with his buttons, and that's when he noticed her body was too hot. Her voice too husky.

"I miss seeing you in your uniform." She paused, traced

her tongue over her lips, and added, "And I miss seeing you out of it."

His teeth clenched. Okay, he knew she was a damn good actress, but Jesus, if he didn't know better, he'd think she was as hot for him as he was for her.

"Your turn," she murmured.

The air around them was charged with sexual energy and he knew if he didn't soon get out of there, he was either going to have his way with her or explode in his increasingly too-tight work pants. She palmed his biceps, and her warm familiar scent drove his need for her to new heights.

She released his top button and his entire body began shaking, everything inside him urging him to take one little nibble. One tiny fucking bite. Her hot hands slipped under his shirt and when her touch went right through him, it was all he could do to marshal his control.

*Breathe, Bennett, breathe.*

Feeling frantic, edgy, so close to losing it, he glanced over her face and the honesty in those honey-flecked eyes of hers pulled him into a place he had no intention of going.

"This…this is where we kiss," she murmured, her voice sounding breathless.

With lust fueling his actions and his brain no longer functioning at full capacity, his mouth closed over hers, and the softness of her lips nearly drove him to his knees. He pressed deeper and kissed her like a man hell-bent on a mission to claim what he wanted. What he needed.

*More.*

Her tongue swept inside his mouth to tangle with his, and he drew it in deeper, craving, demanding.

*So good. So fucking good.*

He pulled her against him, and her breasts felt hot, swollen. She circled her hands around his back, and impatience thrummed through him as her body teased and tormented him in a way no woman's ever had before.

*Need.*

But this was *Eden Carver*!

She was too sweet. Too innocent. And she'd want things he couldn't give her.

*Fuck.*

Nostrils flaring, he worked hard to keep it together as need pushed him to the edge of oblivion. His hands clamped her wrists. Vaguely remembering what he was supposed to do next, he slapped the cuffs on her and pulled her arms over her head. Once he had her captive, he kissed her with fierce possession, everything inside him eager to strip her naked so he could acquaint himself with her body—using his hands, his tongue. His cock.

"Jay." Eagerness laced her voice and some small part of him registered that she'd called him by *his* name.

Teetering on the edge and needing her in a way he'd never needed another, his lips devoured her with rough desire, and as much as he tried, there was nothing he could do to slow down. Savage with the urge to taste every inch of her lush body, he drove his tongue back inside to mate with hers.

Tension rose inside him. He let go of her hands and reached for her shirt, ready to push it from her shoulders, but when she made a noise, he stilled and desperately clawed for a scrap of control before he ravished her right there in the dark alleyway.

"Jay," she murmured again, but he was so far gone, too far lost in her to understand what she was asking of him.

He needed to get it together and he needed to do it now. He fisted her shirt and tried to concentrate on his breathing. Tried to shake the buzz from his head. "Tell me what we're doing."

Her eyes clouded, and keeping her hands over her head, she rolled her hips. "We're winging it."

*Do and say what comes naturally.*

He gulped air, her words unleashing something primal inside him. "You don't want me to go there."

Her voice was a low, intimate whisper when she said, "Maybe I do."

With lust overshadowing sensibility, he put his hands over hers, widened her legs with his knee, and when he felt the heat of her sex on his thigh, he damn near lost it.

"Eden," he whispered.

"Mmm," she said and moved against him.

Despite the fact that they were outside and could get caught at any moment, he groaned without censor. He'd already established that Eden was a great actress, but everything in the way she was moving, gyrating, scraping that hot little pussy against his leg made him wonder if she was still acting. He inched back to see her, and the desire reflecting in her eyes told him everything he needed to know. She wanted him as much as he wanted her. Fierce need raged inside him and his cock pulsed, screaming to plunge inside her.

*Go slow, Bennett, go slow. This is Eden…*

Even though some functioning brain cell was warning him to take it easy, that she didn't know what she was getting herself into with him, his body was urging him to take her.

*Now.*

He kissed her again, his cock pressing so firmly against her sweet spot he was about ready to erupt. His tongue lashed against the inside of her mouth. Hard. Rough. Greedy.

Christ, he'd just lectured himself on taking it slow, but he knew he wasn't being gentle. Not by any means. But the need to be inside her was making him frantic, crazed.

*One bite. One fucking nibble.*

He shouldn't be doing this.

"Tell me to stop. Please, Eden. Tell me to stop."

When silence met his words, a riot of emotions rushed

through him and he buried his face in her neck. Then he did the one thing he swore he wouldn't do. He lightly bit into her soft flesh, and then he used the soft blade of his tongue to soothe the sting he left behind.

*Sweet. So damn sweet.*

She gasped, and he felt a tremble move through her body. In one swift move, his mouth crashed back down on hers and he pushed harder against her. The handcuffs jangled as she reached around his neck. She gripped him tighter as he kissed her harder, deeper, faster.

He slid a hand between her legs, dipped inside her panties, and scraped the soft pad of his thumb over her clit. She cried out, and when she thrust her hips forward the movement nearly obliterated what little control he had left.

He buried his face in her hair and purposely put his mouth close to her ear. "Tell me to slow down and I will," he rasped, before taking a small nibble of her lobe.

Her nails bit into his skin, scratching his flesh in the most seductive ways. He momentarily stilled, because he hadn't expected that. Hadn't expected her to bite back.

Biting back changed everything.

"Jay."

Hearing his name on her lips shattered his last vestige of control. "Yeah?" he asked, his breath coming quicker now.

Needing her naked, he grabbed his key and removed one cuff. Then he slid his hands over her sides and ripped her shirt off her shoulders. He palmed her bare skin before unhooking her bra. He trembled at the sight of her gorgeous breasts, her pert nipples just begging to be sucked.

She opened her mouth to say something, but he slapped the cuff back on and said, "Hands over your head — now."

Her words died an abrupt death and she moaned in bliss.

The second she obliged, his mouth went to her nipple. He licked, sucked, nibbled, and bit into her hard buds until she writhed wildly beneath his mouth. He continued to indulge in her breasts, taking turns to give them both the attention they deserved.

After he'd had his fill, his mouth traveled a path down her body. He sank to his knees, gripped her short skirt, and pushed it up until her sexy panties were exposed. The fragrant tang of her arousal reached his nostrils and he groaned.

He pressed his mouth to the moist juncture between her legs and ran his tongue over the thin lace covering the spot that needed him the most. Jesus, she was wet. So damn hot.

"Oh, God."

The pleasure resonating in her voice licked him from head to toe. As lust tore through him, he curled his finger in the scrap of material and, with one quick tug, tore it from her hips. He shoved her panties into his pocket and without pause widened her wet lips with his fingers, then buried his face between her legs and plunged his tongue in deep.

She bucked against him, her cries of ecstasy cutting the quiet of the night. When he pressed his thumb over her clit, he realized how close she was. He could feel her muscles clenching, spasming, pulsing, screaming for him to take her over the precipice.

He pushed a finger inside and his entire body throbbed when her walls squeezed hard.

*So tight.*

Her breathing changed, coming faster now. Her hips began moving, rocking, driving his finger in and out. In and out.

He added another finger and she clutched his head, her hands fisting his hair, and he knew. Knew she was right there.

"I told you to keep your hands over your head. Now do what I say, or I stop."

The second she lifted her arms, putting herself at his mercy, he punched up the pressure and raked his teeth over her puckered clit, knowing just what she needed to push her over the edge.

"Jay," she cried out, her body quaking beneath his touch as she let herself go.

Her liquid heat singed his mouth and he stayed between her legs for a long time, drawing out her orgasm with his tongue.

Off in the distance, some coherent part of his brain registered the slamming of a car door.

*Shit.*

Knowing he wanted her alone where he could have her all to himself and ravish her with his dark hunger, he climbed to his feet and pulled her skirt down. He quickly removed the cuffs and gathered her blouse. Wrapping it around her shoulders to cover her nakedness, he grabbed her hand and tugged.

Without speaking, he hurried them back to his apartment, and once they were inside, he scooped her into his arms, carried her to his bedroom, and tossed her onto his bed. She blinked up at him as he stood over her, and her beauty took his breath away.

*Mine.*

He noted the color on her cheeks and the heat in her eyes as he made short work of his clothes.

"Get undressed," he commanded in a soft voice.

His eyes swept over her curves and his body shook almost violently as she shimmied out of her clothes and tossed them to the floor. She was about to kick off her sexy shoes, but the shake of his head stopped her. Raw need gathered in the pit of his stomach as he saw her lying there in nothing but those stilettos, and he knew restraint was a thing of the past.

"Open your legs."

When she obliged, he reached into his nightstand, grabbed a condom, and sheathed himself. With her pussy glistening invitingly, he climbed on top of her until she was held captive beneath his weight. He knew this was going to be rough, and he was probably going to leave a bruise or two, but come tomorrow, he wanted her to remember this was real, that he wasn't some imaginary character from her script.

With single-minded determination, he pinned her arms above her head again. Unable to think and only able to feel, his mouth found hers and in one quick, hard thrust, he drove his cock all the way inside her. She gasped and when her warm wet heat wrapped around him, he nearly sobbed with pleasure.

She lifted her hips to meet each thrust, and he was so delirious with want he drove into her harder, faster, fucking her with such a fevered pitch and giving her everything he had inside him that he was sure they were going to break the bed frame and crash to the floor.

With long driving strokes he plunged deeper, seeking, needing, searching for more than just relief.

In no time at all, the air around them grew heavy, and moisture pebbled their bodies as they fucked long and hard. He continued to thrust, desperately trying to assuage the ache inside him, one that had been gnawing at him since the first time he'd set eyes on her.

She moaned, another orgasm pulling at her, and when her wet heat scorched his cock, his whole body began trembling. His throat clenched and his cock tightened to the point of no return as pressure mounted. He'd never felt anything like this. Never felt such intense pleasure.

Such heat.

"Eden…" he whispered, emotions hitting so hard his mind completely shut down.

*Lost. So fucking lost in her.*

Unable to get enough of her, tension coiled through his body and his muscles clenched hard. His mouth found hers as he gave himself over to the pleasure and with a loud moan that reverberated off his walls, he let himself go high inside her. Her hands circled his back and held tight as he collapsed on top of her, wet heat sealing their bodies as one.

A long time later, he pulled out and discarded the condom. He slid in beside her, gathered her soft body into his arms, and covered them both with a bedsheet. As everything inside him screamed possession, he realized she was quiet.

Too quiet.

Jay swallowed and as the lust cleared from his rattled brain, he wondered what the hell he'd just done. His heart squeezed in his too-tight chest and his throat constricted because when it came to Eden, he knew there was a line he wasn't supposed to cross. But not only had he crossed it, he'd jumped up and down on it, pounded it into the ground, and then mocked it.

And in the process, he'd corrupted a sweet and innocent country girl, one who he wanted to give the world but just couldn't.

# Chapter Four

Eden lay there, too astonished to breathe.

Never in her life had sex been that good, that intense. As contentment coiled through her, every muscle in her body ached—in the most beautiful, erotic way. Jay was so wild, so frantic, so passionate and possessive. He was everything she needed him to be.

She turned her head to see him and wanted to say something, but words were completely lost on her. Instead, she just stayed there in his strong arms, listening to his breathing. Even though she was exhausted, she couldn't slow her mind down enough to sleep. All she wanted to do was play out the night's events in her mind over and over again.

Some time later, she turned on her side and stared at the amazing man next to her. As her gaze tracked the rigid muscles on his stomach, her body warmed all over. He looked good in his uniform, but by God, he looked even better out of it.

With his head turned from her, she couldn't see his face, so she took that time to study his magnificent body. When she spotted the tattoo on his arm, she resisted the urge to trace it. She'd seen it before, of course, but she'd never had the courage to ask who Jess was. Perhaps there was some part of her that didn't want to find out, didn't want to know why this particular girl was important enough to warrant a spot on his arm.

But it did make her wonder if he'd been hurt by her. Could she be the reason he couldn't commit? The reason he'd closed off his private life to her? She also couldn't help but wonder what came next for them. She certainly hoped once she proved how good they could be together that he'd want a real relationship with her, but there was a small part of her that was suddenly worried. What if he considered what they'd done another notch on his belt?

Pushing that worry aside and hoping the great time they had would change things for the better, she snuggled in close. The hours ticked by far too quickly for her, because she never wanted this night to end, never wanted to leave the comfort of his bed, his arms. But as morning light peeked into the window, she dozed off, only to be awakened by a ringing phone.

Jay stirred beside her, then reached for the cell phone sitting on his nightstand. Smiling as memories bombarded her, she stretched out her deliciously fatigued limbs and listened to the exchange for a moment. He hung up and turned to her, but when she caught his look, her smile dissolved.

"Everything okay?" she asked, wanting him to open up to her about his work in the hopes that sharing his bad days would make it easier. She knew his job was dangerous, but he was smart, skilled, a warrior who knew how to take care of himself, which helped ease her worries when he was on the streets.

He opened his mouth like he wanted to say something, but then he frowned and said, "The captain needs me. I have to go."

Eden glanced at the clock, her stomach in knots because this was not how she expected her morning to go. Jay seemed a little distant, a little distracted, and she feared it had more to do with her and what had transpired between them than the work call he'd just received.

Trying to play things off as casual, she shrugged and said, "I have to go, too. I'm due on set in a few hours."

He climbed from the bed and she tried not to stare, tried not to feel overwhelmed with emotions when he disappeared into the bathroom. She listened to the shower, then a few minutes later, he was back in his bedroom, pulling on his uniform.

He stood at the foot of the bed and turned to her, and she could feel the strain between them. His eyes met hers. They looked dark, tortured. Regretful.

Eden's stomach dropped as he scrubbed a hand over his chin and said, "Lock up on your way out."

With her voice lodged somewhere in her throat, she simply nodded and tugged the sheet up to her neck.

*Oh, God, what have I done?*

She stayed there for a long time, wondering if she'd made a mistake, one that could very well have cost her a friendship. She wanted Jay, of that she had no doubt. And last night, he'd wanted her, too. Sexually, at least.

But that didn't mean he wanted anything more from her, and perhaps he'd only had sex with her because she really hadn't given him much of a choice.

Then another thought hit. Perhaps he'd caught on that she'd written the script and now that he was aware of her secret desires, she thought she was some sort of freak because she wanted to be tied up, to be held captive, and to enjoy kinky things like spankings and exhibitionism.

Either way, while it might have been the best night of her

life, this morning was turning out to be the worst one she'd ever faced.

Her stomach rebelled, and, needing in the most desperate way to get out of there, she climbed from the bed and pulled on her skirt and ripped blouse. On the floor, she spotted the uniform he'd been wearing last night, her panties, and his cuffs sticking out of the pocket.

As she hurried to the door, a framed picture on his dresser caught her attention. She stopped for a brief moment to take a look and that's when she realized she'd never actually been in his bedroom before last night. When she spotted a young girl holding a cake that said *Happy Sixteenth Jess*, her heart went into her throat, because she knew from the resemblance that Jess was Jay's sister.

Her mind raced and as sadness welled up inside her, she understood there was so much more to this man's life than she knew, so much more than he'd let her see. With the way he tore out of here earlier, she was pretty certain he'd only ever wanted her friendship, but she'd screwed things up so badly he might not even want that anymore.

• • •

With his work day over, Jay maneuvered his Jeep through the Friday evening traffic and thought more about his night with Eden. She'd wanted him. Of that, he was certain. Hell, he'd wanted her, too. Which, truth be told, was the reason he hadn't been with another woman in weeks. How could he possibly bed someone else when his thoughts were completely preoccupied with Eden?

But he'd let her down.

He'd let himself down.

He went at her the way he knew he would. Like a goddamn animal.

She was sweet and innocent and deserved soft and slow. What she didn't deserve was a man who wanted to fuck as hard as he worked. A man who needed to let off a little steam after a rough day on the beat.

A man who couldn't give her what she'd want.

*Shit.*

But now that they'd crossed a line and had taken their relationship to a whole new level, he knew they couldn't go back. Everything had changed, including their friendship, and he needed to figure out what the hell he was going to do about it, because he damn well wasn't about to lose her. He drove around the city a little longer, trying to figure out how to make this right. He wanted her in his life, of that much he was certain, but how could he have her and continue to honor his sister's memory? While he wasn't certain about the latter, he knew he needed to start in the bedroom and at least make that part right between them.

By the time he reached his condo it was late, well past the time he usually checked in on Eden. But it would still be a bit longer because he had a stage to set.

He hurried inside his place and after he had everything arranged, he hopped in the shower to scrub the streets from his skin. Once clean, he pulled on a pair of jeans and a T-shirt and padded barefoot across the hall. He listened outside her door for a moment and for some odd reason hoped she was just on the other side of the door, listening back.

He rapped softly and waited to hear her footsteps. But when they didn't come, he knocked again. That's when her door inched open.

As soon as he set eyes on her, his heart started beating faster, and it took all his restraint not to pull her in tight and plant a hungry kiss on her mouth. He took a second to look her over and noted she was dressed in a silk nightie; the warm flush on her cheeks toyed with his resolve. His cock thickened and he fisted his hands, because everything inside him urged to pull her into his arms and ravage the hell out of her.

"Hey," he said, trying to keep it together, because he was not about to take her the way he wanted to, he reminded himself. Not ever again.

"Hey," she said back. Then she narrowed her eyes, concern moving over her face. "Are you okay?"

"I'm okay," he said, although he was anything but, because if he didn't fix this between them, he feared he'd never be okay again.

Disappointment moved over her face. "I know you're not—"

"Can you come over for a minute?"

She looked at him for a moment, then said, "Let me grab my slippers." She glanced around her apartment. "Now if I could only remember where I put them."

"Just put those on," he said, pointing toward the sexy shoes she wore last night.

She gave him an odd look before saying, "Okay."

He captured her hand in his and swallowed hard, trying not to notice how long and sexy her legs looked in those shoes as he ushered her across the hall and into his condo. Once inside, he closed the door behind them.

He sucked in air, and when she turned to face him, looking like a soft, sexy, well-fucked woman, his throat dried. "Drink?" he asked.

She nodded and concern moved over her face as she looked at him. "Why don't I get it?" she said, gesturing for him to sit on the sofa. "You look like you've had a hard day."

"I'm okay," he said.

"I know you're not," she said, a hardness in her tone that he'd never heard before.

She pushed past him and went into his kitchen, where he had everything prepared for their evening. He watched her pull open the fridge, bend forward, and grab two beers from the bottom.

The sight of her sweet little ass lifted in the air in such a provocative manner evoked a myriad of sinful thoughts and there wasn't a damn thing he could to do purify them. She wiggled slightly, and it bombarded him with primal hunger, complicating his mission to take things slow when all he wanted to do was give her a nice long spanking, then fuck her hard.

*Get it together, Bennett.*

She turned to him, and that's when she noticed the table. "Jay?" she asked, her eyes wide as she took in the candles waiting to be lit and a table set for two.

"Eden," he bit out, barely able to keep the need inside him under lock for another second. Not after she'd unleashed the beast in him last night.

Her chest heaved, and the creamy swell of her breasts nearly rendered him senseless. The air around them charged and tension grew in his body. His cock swelled, everything about her seducing his senses, and there was nothing he could do to bank his desires. He drew in a shaky breath in an attempt to center himself, but there was no denying that he wanted her again. Right here. Right now.

He tried to tamp down his desires, but his cock refused to obey, and before he realized what he was doing, he crossed the room, slipped his arm around her back, and roughly tugged her to him.

"Jay," she rushed out, her eyes alive with anticipation as her flesh suffused with color. "Are you okay?" she asked, her warm breath scorching his skin and raising his need for her to new heights.

"I need to fuck you." He raked a shaky hand through her hair to push it off her face, and when he saw desire reflected in her eyes and understood how much she wanted him again, he said, "I need to fuck you so badly."

"Then what's stopping you?" she asked and shifted her stance until his cock was once again aligned with her pussy.

With his composure slipping, he backed up toward the table, dragging her with him. With one clean swoop, he cleared the top, letting the candles and plates crash to the floor.

"Oh, God," she panted, but his mouth covered hers and swallowed her gasp of surprise as he picked her clear up off the floor. Heat arced between them as he laid her out on the table and climbed on top of her. Pinning her beneath him, his mouth moved urgently over hers, seeking, searching, hungering to taste and claim every inch of her.

His hands shaped her contours, and she quivered beneath him when he drove a knee between her legs to widen them.

"Eden," he whispered, struggling to draw in air.

She ripped at his shirt, her hands rushing over his skin. "Please," she whispered, her soft sexy plea pushing him over the edge.

Feeling shaky and out of control, he tore open her silk nightie, his glance moving to her breasts as the buttons clattered to the floor. His mouth salivated and he groaned at the beautiful sight of her nakedness. Eager for a taste, he drew a nipple into his mouth and slipped a hand between her legs to stroke her wet heat through her damp panties.

No longer able to think and only able to feel, he murmured, "So wet…so damn wet and ready."

She lifted her pelvis and pushed against his fingers, conveying her desires without words, but he needed to hear her say it. "Tell me. Tell me what you want."

She looked straight into his eyes. "I want you to fuck me."

With that, Jay climbed from the table, ripped off his pants and shirt, and then grabbed a condom from his back pocket before he let his clothes fall to the floor. He lowered himself onto the chair and crooked a finger.

Eden sat up on the table, her legs spread wide, giving him a perfect view of her sweet pussy. Want clawed at him as he pushed the thin silk aside to expose her beautiful silken lips, then drove one finger all the way up inside her to test her readiness.

Unbridled desire danced in her eyes as she groaned, her lust-saturated voice making him crazed with the need to fuck her. "So good."

He pulled her lips open and her clit hardened as he swiped his thumb over it. She reached out to grab his shoulders, her body trembling from head to toe. His cock throbbed, aching to be back inside her as she offered herself up so nicely to him.

He pulled his finger out and her groan of disappointment turned into a moan of pleasure as he gripped her panties to pull them down her legs. Leaving her shoes in place, he tossed the panties to the floor and widened her legs to take a good long look at her pink sweetness.

His nostrils flared as he pulled her rich scent into his lungs and it was all he could do to hang on as he tore open the condom to sheathe himself.

"Come here," he ordered, gripping her hips to drag her to him. He pulled her off the table until she was straddling his lap. Eyes full of urgent need moved over his, and a storm began brewing inside him as he lifted her until his cock breached her hot opening.

"Take me," she said, and with that, he powered upward, lunging so deep inside her, he could hear the air leave her lungs.

She cried out and scratched her nails over his back, her hair flying around her face as she tossed her head from side to side. The depth of his penetration and the way her pussy wrapped so tightly around him nearly had him coming upon impact.

He bit down on the inside of his mouth when she began moving, gyrating, taking what she needed from him. Blood pulsing hot, he rammed into her and her mouth opened, but no sound came. He found her clit again, brushed his thumb over it, and she grew slicker with every stroke.

A low growl of longing sounded deep in his throat as she pushed her nipple into his mouth. Blindsided by lust, he sucked, then bit down hard, clamping his teeth around her marbled bud until her moans of pleasure merged with his. His fingers swirled through her thick heat and he could feel her tension mounting.

Pleasure swamped him when she began moving faster, and he gripped her hips to hold on. She rocked forward, scraping her clit over his pelvis, giving the hard nub the stimulation she needed to push herself over the edge.

A whimper escaped her lips when Jay whispered, "You are so hot."

Her fingers slid into his hair, and as he sank into her slick core, her body shuddered, pressing against him, seeking what it craved. When he felt that first erotic pulse, her body clenching and throbbing with the hot flow of release, his world tilted on its axis, every nerve in his body alive and on fire.

"That's it," he said between gritted teeth. "Fuck me hard, baby." Her heat turned him inside out and he pumped harder, scraping his cock over the sensitive bundle of nerves inside her pussy. As he drew out her orgasm, she cried his name and he was sure he'd never seen a more beautiful sight than her coming undone for him.

Intense pleasure forked through him, and as his body went up in flames, blood flowed thick and heavy in his veins. He groaned as her pussy gripped him hard. With actions ruled by lust and needing to answer the urgent demands of his body, he grabbed her shoulders and hauled her down hard on him, driving his cock impossibly deeper. She let loose a whimper, her nails clawing at his skin almost frantically.

As he ravaged her, she moved against him, both giving and taking as they chased release. She whimpered and her eyes turned glossy. The second he felt her climax around him again, he gave a low moan of satisfaction and let go, depleting himself in her.

"Jay," she murmured between breaths as they clung to each other. "Oh my God."

He exhaled slowly and swallowed down the knot pushing into his throat as her labored words resonated inside him. They held on to each other for a long time, and once his breathing returned to normal, reality inched its way into his brain. That's when he realized what he'd done, how hard and rough he'd taken her. Again. He pressed his palm to his forehead, disgusted with himself in so many ways.

He closed his eyes in distress. "Oh shit, shit, shit."

Her hands cupped his face to bring his attention back to her. When he blinked his eyes open and saw confusion written all over her face, his heart dropped into his stomach.

Her body tightened. "What's wrong?"

He pulled out of her and waved his hand around the kitchen. "This. Everything."

There was so much emotion on her face that when her sad eyes met his, it felt like a punch to the gut. "I don't get it."

He took a moment to digest her words, then gave a shake of his head. "I didn't do right by you."

"What are you talking about?"

"I went at you hard, when I swore I'd never do that again." He watched the pulse at the base of her neck pick up tempo. He looked at the mess on his floor. "This is what I want for you. This is what you deserve."

Her brow furrowed and she climbed off his lap. "Who says I want that?"

He gripped her elbow and drew her back. "I was trying to

be the guy you need, at least in the bedroom."

"What makes you think you're not?" Dark lashes blinked over expressive amber eyes, and turmoil grew inside him.

He quickly disposed of the condom, then took her hand to guide her to the sofa, needing to make this right. He sat on the coffee table across from her. "You're a nice girl and I'm a cop who lives a dangerous life. One I want to protect you from. Bad shit happens in my world on a daily basis. Things I don't want you to know about."

"But I want to know about it," she bit out, frustration lacing her normally calm voice. "Don't you see? I want you to share your day with me. I want to be there to help you cope with all the bad things that happen."

"Eden, listen—"

"No, you listen." She gave a hard shake of her head, her blond curls flaring around her face. "I don't know why everyone has the idea that farm girls are delicate beings who chase butterflies and pick daisies. I was driving a tractor at ten years old, and I'm a lot tougher than you think." She blew out a long breath, and her voice softened, becoming unusually low when she added, "I didn't break last night, did I? Or just now?"

Jay cringed. "I never should have gone at you like that. But I've wanted you for so fucking long now, and the truth is, sometimes after a hard day, I need to let off a little steam. But it won't happen again." He dropped his gaze to the floor. "It won't."

"That's too bad."

His head came up with a start. "Too bad? What are you talking about?"

"Yeah, because I want it to happen again."

He shook his head, trying to make sense of what she was saying. "No, you need a guy who can make slow, passionate love to you. I'll try to be that guy you need in the bedroom, but I can't…" He paused and his words fell off. After a long moment, he rubbed the tattoo on his arm and continued with, "I just don't know how to be the guy you need outside of sex."

With everything in the way she was looking at him, he suddenly had the uneasy feeling that she knew. Knew why being on the streets was so important to him.

She grabbed his hand and pulled it into her lap. "Tell me something."

"What?"

"Tell me about Jess."

Air left his lungs in a whoosh and he tried to pull his hand back but she wouldn't let him. "Eden—"

She gave a reassuring squeeze and as her heat moved through him, he felt something inside him give. Her voice was so soft, so low when she asked, "What happened to her?"

"It was a long time ago."

"I still want to know. I want you to open up. I want to help you with the pain."

A long moment passed between them, but when he realized she wasn't about to give up, he moved to the couch and leaned into her, needing her touch in the most unfathomable ways. "She died when we were teenagers and I wasn't there to protect her," he finally admitted, suddenly so tired of keeping it inside, bottled up in a place that tied him in knots and turned his world inside out. But as soon as the words left his mouth, as soon as he shared them with the girl he wanted to make a future with, he felt a new lightness inside him. A new kind of relief.

"Jay," she said. "I'm so sorry, but these are the things I want you to share with me. Things I want to help you deal with. I want to be there for you. To celebrate the good and help you through the bad."

He swallowed and suddenly needed to tell her more, to get it all out so it could no longer eat him up inside. The truth was, he loved Jess and missed her fiercely, but maybe it was time to let go of the pain. "She was in the wrong place at the wrong time. Got caught in the crossfire during a gang shootout."

"And that's why you became a cop? To protect the innocent?"

"Yeah," he said, realizing how astute she was, how much she really did know about him. "It's important for me to be on the streets, to honor her memory."

"I love that you want to protect me from your world. And I love that you're honoring your sister's memory. I'm so glad you're on the streets because they need you."

"Wait, what are you talking about?"

She gave him an odd look. "I'm saying the streets need you."

Confused and guessing she wanted him to choose the streets over her, he gripped her hand hard and asked, "What are you saying?"

"I'm saying I want to be a part of that life with you and that I need you exactly the way you are."

"But I thought you'd want me off the streets."

Looking like she just had an epiphany, she said, "And that's why you always kept things platonic between us."

"You're a sweet farm girl. Danger hasn't been a part of your world."

She gave a slow shake of her head. "Listen. There are lots of dangers on the farm. It's just dangerous in different ways."

"And, well, I didn't want to do something to ruin our friendship. I couldn't handle not having you in my life."

"Jay."

"Yeah."

"I have a confession."

He crooked his head, his stomach tightening. "A confession? What are you talking about?"

"I wrote the script."

With so much going on inside him, he had a hard time trying to sort through what she was saying. "What script?"

"The one I asked you to rehearse with me last night."

Hardly able to believe what he was hearing, his heart began pounding, the room fading in and out of existence. "You did? Why?"

"Because I wanted you to notice me."

He shook his head. "I've always noticed you."

"But you never did anything about it."

"I wanted to."

"And I wanted you to know the *real* me, because you're the man I want in my life." She let loose a slow breath. "I was pretty scared for a while there. Not only did I think I'd ruined our friendship, which is the last thing I ever wanted to do, and that maybe you had no interest in settling down, I was worried that you thought I was some sort of sexual deviant and that's why you flew out of here so fast this morning."

"I flew out of here because I thought *I* fucked things up and wasn't sure how I could be the guy you needed."

She gave him a sexy grin. "Oh, you fucked things up all right."

Heat moved through him and he didn't miss what she was saying as he thought about the roles they'd played. He shook his head and grinned, loving this side of her. "So you have a uniform fetish, then?"

"Among others," she admitted.

"Handcuffs?"

"Uh-huh."

"BDSM, spankings? So I guess when you said it was like the character was written for me, it really was."

"Yeah, it was."

As he thought things through, it occurred to him that not only was he the guy she wanted and needed outside the bedroom, he was the guy she needed inside it as well. His heart swelled as he brushed his thumb along her jaw. "And the alleyway? You've got a thing for outdoors?"

She gave him a sheepish smile and said, "You see, I took a chance and shared something very private with you. Something I never thought I'd ever share with another guy. But I want a real relationship with you and in order for that to happen, I needed you to know who I really am inside."

"I want a relationship with you, too."

She poked him in the chest. "Good, and now I want to know everything about you. If we're going to give this thing between us a shot, you have to open up to me and share your day, even the bad parts." She paused for a moment and looked at him long and hard before asking, "Do you think you could do that?"

He nodded, his mind focused on one thing and one thing only, and there was nothing he could do to hide his crooked grin when he asked, "So you really wrote the script?"

She chuckled. "Yeah, I did." She nibbled on her bottom lip and questioned, "So you don't think my fetishes are deviant?"

"Hell yeah, I do."

She gave him a nervous look and he pulled her to her feet. Their bodies collided and when his thickening cock pressed against her sweet spot, she gasped.

"But Jesus Christ, there is nothing sexier than a sweet farm girl with fetishes." When her eyes lit up, he glanced around his apartment.

"What are you looking for?"

"A pen and paper."

She crinkled her nose. "What for?"

"Because sweetheart, you're not the only one with secrets."

Her eyes widened with equal measures of shock and delight. "I'm not?"

"Hell no. And I'm really anxious to get started on a few of mine." He looked back at her and when he noticed the warm flush crawling up her neck, he asked, "Do you think you're up for it?"

She grinned, aligning her hips with his so she was pressing against his hard erection, and when she said, "I know *you* are," his heart soared like a leaf caught in an updraft. Because he knew as long as he had sweet and sexy Eden in his arms, his bed, and his life, his future was going to be a very bright and happy one.

Not to mention a deliciously naughty one.

# About the Author

A multi published author in the romance genre, Cathryn is a wife, mom, sister, daughter, and friend. She loves dogs, sunny weather, anything chocolate (she never says no to a brownie), pizza, and red wine. She has two teenagers who keep her busy with their never-ending activities and a husband who is convinced he can turn her into a mixed martial arts fan. Cathryn can never find balance in her life; is always trying to find time to go to the gym; can never keep up with e-mails, Facebook, or Twitter; and tries to write page-turning books her readers will love.

A maritimer at heart and former financial officer, Cathryn has lived all over Canada but has finally settled down in her childhood hometown with her family.

www.cathrynfox.com

Made in United States
Cleveland, OH
08 May 2025